D0674343

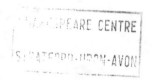

THE STORY OF
The THEATRE

by L. DU GARDE PEACH, M.A., PhD., D.Litt.
with illustrations by MARTIN AITCHISON

Ladybird Books Loughborough

THE STORY OF THE THEATRE

All children like playing games: if they have to dress
up as somebody else to play these games, they like them
even better. Sometimes they are cowboys and Indians,
sometimes 'cops and robbers', but almost always they
are acting the parts of good people against bad people.
In other words: there is some sort of conflict.

The theatre exists today because dressing-up is something which everybody likes doing, even when they are
grown up.

The people whom we call 'primitive' were very like
children. They could not read or write, of course. Even
when they talked together, their language consisted of
very few words. But they could draw animals and men
on the walls of their caves, and they could act stories
about hunting or fighting with their enemies. So when
a primitive man came home after killing a cave bear,
he did not try to tell his family or tribe about it: he
acted it. Perhaps sometimes he would get a friend to
put on the skin of a bear, and it made the story of the
fight much more real.

If the two men were good actors, they found that
everybody wanted to see the story of the bear, and they
had to act it over and over again. In time they had done
it so often that they always acted it in the same way.
Their story of the killing of the cave bear had become a
mime play.

4   *Cave-men mime a bear-hunt.*

If the mime play was very good, with a lot of running about and shouting, perhaps the two primitive men would teach it to their sons. They in turn would teach it to *their* sons, and perhaps hundreds of years later, the descendants of the first two men would still be acting the play of how the bear was hunted and killed.

But something would have happened to the play in the meantime. Little bits of what in the theatre is called 'business' would have been added, and perhaps some long-forgotten actor would have introduced something to make people laugh. Possibly the actor dropped his flint-headed spear, and turned and ran away with the bear after him. He found that if he fell down a few times and the bear nearly caught him, everybody laughed even more. So every time the play was acted, the actor always dropped his spear, and was nearly caught by the bear.

When the mime of the hunting of the bear became even more popular, some particular place and time was chosen for its performance. This might well have been a piece of flat ground at the foot of a hill on which the audience could sit and watch.

This was really the first theatre, though of course primitive man never called it that: he could have had no idea that his simple game would develop into the theatre of today. But that is exactly what happened.

Primitive man discovers how to make people laugh.

In the course of hundreds of years, the running about in the mime plays of fighting or the hunting of animals became dances. Such dances may still be seen amongst savage tribes living in forests or in deserts. Often the skins of animals, and fearsome masks of their heads, are worn by the dancers.

The next step in the long history of the theatre was when wooden platforms were built for the dancers. The stories now represented heroes of past ages, and were developed in Greece more than 2,500 years ago. Then, 500 years before the Christian era, there came the next great stride forward: the actors and dancers began to speak and sing.

There is one name which anyone interested in the theatre ought to know and remember, the name of the first great dramatist of whom we know: Aeschylus*, born in the year 525 B.C. in Eleusis in a part of Greece then known as Attica.

The first permanent theatre of stone was probably built before 400 B.C. It was still on a convenient hillside, on which were stone steps for the audience. The area for the dancers became a circle, called the *orkestra* and behind it was a low stage for the actors, on which was built a changing room or *skene*. The front of the skene was later to become decorated and from it came our word scene.

There were never more than three players on the stage at any one time, and, as these theatres were in the open air, and sometimes seated 30,000 people, the actors wore masks with small speaking trumpets inside them to magnify their voices.

An early Greek theatre.
(Inset) A mask of an old man.
*Aeschylus: pronounced Ees-killus.

8

Wonderful ruins of Greek theatres are still to be seen at places like Athens and Epidaurus, and when the Romans started building theatres, they copied those of Greece. In Italy and France, and even in England at St. Albans, the Roman town of Verulamium, we can see the remains of Roman theatres. With a little imagination we can picture what it must have been like with the stone steps seating hundreds of people, and the actors performing on the shallow stage.

The Romans, who were very practical people, changed the general form of the theatre. The round orchestra, where the Greek chorus had performed religious dances, became much smaller and finally disappeared. The stage was increased in size to accommodate more actors, and the plays often dealt with ordinary people, instead of telling the stories of gods and heroes.

Perhaps even more important was the fact that the Romans introduced a curtain across the front of the stage. This did not open or rise as it does in most theatres today: it fell down into a sort of trench. It could not be raised again, but it meant that some sort of scenery could be hidden from the audience until the play was ready to begin. The Greeks had used cranes to lower the actors playing the parts of gods from above, or to raise those playing warriors to Olympus, where the gods lived. The Romans added trap-doors and other mechanical devices, and sometimes an awning which could be drawn over the audience to protect them in bad weather.

Above: The remains of a Roman theatre at St. Albans, and
Below: An artist's reconstruction of this theatre.

When the barbarians came down from the north in the sixth century and destroyed the civilisation of Rome, the theatre virtually disappeared. The actors were all out of work. In order to make a living, they took to the roads of Europe, performing mimes or simple plays at fairs, or wherever a few people were gathered together.

For hundreds of years this was the only kind of theatrical entertainment in western Europe. The minstrels of France and the gleemen of England kept alive the love of simple shows. Often these were long and rather dull tales of adventure, sung by a single performer; occasionally two or more men would travel together and perform rough comedy scenes.

The gleemen who came to England with the Saxon and Danish invaders recited tales of heroic battles and adventures to the accompaniment of a sort of harp. A long and occasionally exciting poem called 'Beowulf', performed about the year 600, is the oldest example of such an entertainment.

It was not until the eleventh century that the minstrels were made welcome in the castles of the noblemen of France and Norman England. They were highly skilled entertainers, and one of them, Rahere, at the court of Henry I, became so rich that he founded a priory. Then something happened which was very important in the history of the theatre. Previously the Church had frowned on the wandering minstrels, and had persecuted them. Then a change gradually occurred.

12   *The minstrels' songs were sometimes long and rather dull.*

In the tenth century only a very few people in England, apart from the priests, could read or write. There were no books as we know them. Printing had not yet been invented, and every book had to be written by hand.

In the churches all the services were in Latin, which the common people could not understand. But when a simple play was acted in English in the market place, everybody went to see it, and everybody understood it.

The men and boys who acted such plays were known as rogues and vagabonds and often set in the stocks on the village green. But the priests saw that the people all enjoyed them, so they decided that it would be a very good way to teach the stories of the saints, and the parables and stories of the Bible, to simple people.

The Christian Church had very early begun to stage what were really only tableaux, without movement or spoken words, in the churches. A thousand years ago, just as in many churches today, a crib would be set up in the chancel at Christmas, or a little scene showing the Sepulchre at Easter. There were sometimes a few simple questions and answers. The three kings or the shepherds were represented by priests, or some of the nuns would be dressed as angels, with tinsel wings. Gradually more little scenes were added, staged in different parts of the church.

A simple Christmas play in mediaeval times.

Very soon there was not room in the churches for all the people who wished to see the plays. The only thing to do was to present them outside the churches, on the entrance steps. The time soon came when the priests and the nuns could no longer satisfy the demand, and the task of presenting the plays was handed over to the craft guilds.

By the twelfth century the people of the country had already banded themselves together under their particular trades to form guilds. The cutlers, the goldsmiths, the tailors, and so on, all had their separate trade associations, many of which remain to this day.

When the guilds took over the performance of the plays, they often chose the story best suited to their particular craft. The shipwrights acted the story of Noah, the builders the erection of Solomon's Temple, the tailors the story of Joseph and the coat of many colours. Special stages were built round the market place and the audience moved from one to the other, seeing the scenes in the proper order. Apart from the plays of stories from the Bible, known as Mystery plays, there were also Miracle plays about the saints, and Morality plays, invented stories using imaginary characters to show the struggle between Good and Evil.

The players from the guilds were what we would today call amateurs: soon the professionals – the 'rogues and vagabonds' – came on the scene.

16

The craftsmen's guilds present their plays in the market place.

The religious plays were presented on special occasions only, but the professionals played all the year round. Wherever they could raise an audience, they set up some sort of a stage and sounded drums and trumpets to gather people together.

As they were still looked upon by the authorities as undesirables, they were not able to set up semi-permanent stages in the market place. Instead, they mounted their scenes on waggons and moved them from one street corner to another, blowing their trumpets as they went.

A man who actually saw all this hundreds of years ago, wrote down a description of it. This, with his spelling, is what he saw:

"...a highe place made like a howse with two rowmes, being open on ye tope: the lower rowme they apparrelled and dressed them selves; and in the higher rowme they played: and they stood upon 6 wheeles."

The professionals played some of the more popular religious plays, such as 'Everyman', but for the most part they acted what were called 'merrie conceits'. These were knock-about comedies or farces with a lot of action and broad humour. All the acting of the women's characters was undertaken by men or boys, but often the settings were very realistic. When the players wished to show the place of punishment for the wicked, they built a big dragon's mouth, out of which came fire and smoke.

The professionals perform their play on top of a waggon.
18   *A dragon's mouth represents Hell.*

Then two things happened, both very important in the development of the English theatre. The wandering professionals ceased to use their waggons, and began acting in the open courtyards of the inns. These were much more suitable than waggons in the market place. Up and down the country – at Gloucester for example – these old courtyards are still to be seen. Often they have been roofed over with glass, but it is easy to imagine what they must have looked like when the players came to town.

Most of these old inns had an open gallery round the courtyard at first floor level. Here the richer people could sit in comfort and watch the play. Standing in the courtyard below were the artisans and apprentices, who were at times very noisy and unruly. It was the task of the players to make them listen: if the play was good enough, they often succeeded.

The second important thing was the change in the way in which plays were produced and performed.

Always in the long history of the theatre, authors have written plays to suit the stages on which they hoped that they would be performed. In Ancient Greece and Rome the stages were open to the sky, and the auditorium often held thousands of people: in mediaeval England the stages were also without roofs, but the audiences were much smaller and nearer to the actors.

20   *A play in progress in an inn courtyard, showing the gallery.*

When the players moved to the courtyards of the inns, it meant that better educated people came to watch them. This produced a demand for more intelligent plays. Many educated men from the universities, who would have scorned the rough action and dialogue of the 'merrie conceits', now began to write for the stage.

The inns were places of importance. For hundreds of years, until the coming of the railways, they were not only places of refreshment but also the stopping places for the stage coaches covering the country. They were very busy places, and sometimes the actors had to wait until there was a lull in the traffic. Gradually the plays began to pay the innkeeper better than the stage coaches, and some of the old courtyards became more or less regular theatres.

The courtyards were often large enough to hold three hundred people or more. As they paid a penny or twopence each, this added up to quite a lot of money in those days when a horse and cart, together with the carter, could be hired for twopence a day.

It became the practice for the innkeeper to take the money paid by the nobles or people of quality for the seats in the balcony, the players receiving only the takings from the courtyard. Not only were the players and audience more comfortable, it became much more difficult for unscrupulous persons to see the show without paying.

An audience pays to enter a courtyard theatre.

Some of the players and innkeepers became comparatively rich, but it was at the Royal Court that almost unlimited money was available for the production of plays and masques. Particularly was this the case under Queen Elizabeth and the Stuarts.

Plays which were written for production at the Court were very different from the early entertainments in the market places. They demanded dancing and the lovely music of the period. Above all, the courtiers loved a spectacle. The man who early in the seventeenth century introduced into England what is called the picture frame stage and elaborate scenery, was an architect named Inigo Jones.

More money could be and often was spent on the scenery for one production at the Court than was earned by a whole company of strolling players in a year. Beautiful scenes were built and painted. Those of the forest glades, and particularly the scenes representing palaces, had to be good enough to match the surroundings when set up in St. James's Palace or Windsor Castle.

The people of London were very fond of large pageants and gorgeously dressed processions through the streets of London. When Elizabeth I went to Westminster to tell the Members of Parliament what they must do and say, it was a very colourful cavalcade which the people enjoyed seeing. All this influenced the players, of course. They had to try to give their audiences a more colourful show than they could see for nothing in the streets of London.

24

A royal procession, possibly with dancers and tumblers or acrobats, passing through a London street.

The reign of the Queen who loved the theatre saw also the beginnings of the men who hated it – the Puritans – who fifty years later were to close the theatres altogether. The corporations of many towns and cities, including London, were controlled by Puritans, and the acting of plays was forbidden. Fortunately things were different at Stratford-upon-Avon. Many of the companies of players, driven out of London, visited the quiet little market town where a young man, named Will Shakespeare, was in his teens.

At this time the plague broke out regularly in London. Each main street had an open sewer running down the middle, and the plague – with innumerable rats to spread it – was always a danger. As it was highly infectious, any gatherings like theatre audiences were not permitted within the city walls.

Outside them it was different. Here there were fewer rats and no crowded streets, and it was here that a stage-struck carpenter saw his chance to build a wooden theatre. This theatre was outside the control of the Lord Mayor of London, but near enough for Londoners to visit it. It was so popular that other theatres were built by other companies. Soon there were five or six, and the interesting thing about them is that they were built like the courtyards of the inns but without the inns. The design of theatres today is still based on the inn courtyards of hundreds of years ago.

Theatres of Shakespeare's time on the south bank of the River Thames.

The galleries round the courtyards had been necessary to enable the guests staying at the inn to get to the bedrooms, the doors of which opened onto them. The theatres being built during the time of Queen Elizabeth, and up to the outbreak of the Civil War, imitated the inn courtyards: the galleries remained, but there were of course no bedrooms. In the next century these galleries developed into the 'dress circle', so named because members of the audience were expected to wear evening-dress when occupying them.

The plays of Ancient Greece and Rome required theatres of a particular size and shape, and all the plays of classical times were written to be performed in them. There is no profit in writing plays for which no suitable theatre exists. The first plays which Shakespeare ever saw were acted on an open Elizabethan stage, and because he wrote plays to make money, he wrote them to suit the stages and theatres of his day.

In an old inn, the bedrooms were built all round the central courtyard, and as the gallery was the only way of getting to them, it also went all round. Therefore when the players put up a temporary stage along one side of the courtyard, the gallery was across the back of it. They were obliged to tolerate it because it was there, and there was no way of getting rid of it for one or two nights. Then they found that because it was above the level of their heads, it could be very useful.

On a stage with no scenery, it could be the upper window of a house, the battlements of a castle, or a balcony: Shakespeare used it frequently.

The balcony scene from 'Romeo and Juliet'.

The theatres in Shakespeare's time must have been very uncomfortable, draughty, wet in bad weather and cold in winter. There were often no seats in the pit, so called originally because it was similar to the pit in which bears were set to fight with dogs. It was open to the sky, only a part of the stage being roofed over. The galleries were little better. They admitted all the weather on the side towards the stage, although they were protected from the rain by a roof of tiles or thatch.

There was no heating. One of the later theatres, the Blackfriars in the City of London, was entirely protected by a roof, and a few open braziers burning charcoal may have raised the temperature a few degrees. Otherwise the audience must have suffered severely in the climate of Elizabethan England.

It is therefore not surprising that the audiences in Shakespeare's day were noisy, rough, and without any consideration for the actors or one-another. There were no police, and it was no-one's duty to keep order. If the play and the players did not hold the attention of the audience sufficiently to keep them quiet, their behaviour frequently put an abrupt end to the performance.

Shakespeare was fighting against the conditions of the theatres in which his plays were performed: that he successfully overcame them shows what a genius he was.

The audience at Shakespeare's Globe Theatre had little protection from the weather.

With the victory of the Parliamentary forces in the Civil War, the history of the theatre in England becomes virtually a blank for almost twenty years. Cromwell was fond of music, and he liked simple country dancing on the village greens, but he and all the Puritans looked on the theatre as utterly wicked.

Although in England the playhouses were closed and many of them demolished, the far more advanced theatres of Paris and Bruges were open and flourishing. King Charles and his followers were living in exile in France and, with little to occupy his time, there can be no doubt that visits to the theatre were among his chief pleasures.

In 1660, King Charles II returned to a country starved of beauty and entertainment. He brought with him not only a love of the theatre, but also the determination to see it flourishing in England once again.

The old un-roofed playhouses of Shakespeare's day were no longer in use. But there were still some of the old actors alive, and when a theatre was built in Drury Lane and a covered tennis court in Lincolns Inn Fields was fitted with a stage, there was no shortage of players. What is more, Shakespeare's god-son, Sir William Davenant, who had written and produced plays under Charles I, had during the Cromwellian period been able to stage plays in the houses of noblemen far from London.

Sir William Davenant welcomes Charles II to a performance of a masque in a nobleman's house.

There was another very important difference between the old playhouses of Elizabeth I and the new theatres of Charles II: for the first time in England women appeared on the stage. During his final two or three years abroad, Charles had seen the early comedies of Molière, a French playwright, in which women regularly took part. He was determined that women should take the female rôles in England.

The fact that the audience and the players were both now under cover meant that plays were performed by artificial light. All performances had of necessity to be during daylight hours in the open-roofed theatres of Elizabethan times: they could now take place at any time of the day or night.

The interior of the new theatre was a combination of some of the features of the pre-Civil War stage and others which we should recognise as being still in use. The proscenium, which is the frame up the sides and above the front of the stage, and the curtain were similar to those of today, but the stage was extended out into the audience. On each side of this extension there were boxes, used sometimes by the audience, sometimes by the players. The extended stage was necessary because the lighting was very poor. The curtain came with the use of painted scenery. On the old, open stage there had been nothing to hide, except an occasional throne or some other piece of furniture. For this purpose, a small curtain sometimes hung from the gallery at the back of the stage.

Nell Gwyn on the Drury Lane stage.

The next two hundred years saw little change in the general form of the theatre itself. The apron, as the projection into the audience was called, gradually disappeared. It was in any case outside the proscenium arch, and became less necessary when lighting improved.

Such changes as took place were in the equipment of the stage and the auditorium, the name given to the part of the theatre occupied by the audience. Here more comfort was demanded as the audience changed in character and ceased to be largely made up of the rough, unruly types of Shakespeare's time. Now it consisted of the more wealthy, though often not better mannered, members of the new aristocracy.

Scenery became more elaborate and better painted. But strangely enough, though the scenery was often designed to represent a past century, the costumes of the actors were as a rule those of their own day. Hamlet was played by the famous actor Betterton in 1670 in the huge periwig of the period of Charles II.

In the diary of a man named Samuel Pepys we have very vivid descriptions of what the theatre was like between the return of Charles II in 1660 and the end of the diary in 1669. Mr. Pepys was a great theatre-goer, and was often behind the scenes with the actors and actresses. From him we also learn that the seats at the theatre were not numbered and reserved, but servants were allowed to keep them for their masters.

Mr. Pepys behind the scenes at Drury Lane.

One description of the theatre of this period, written in 1770 when George III was on the throne, tells of the rush for the best seats when the doors were opened. These seats were often benches with no backs to them, and everybody climbed over them to get to the front. As the women all wore large, hooped skirts, they were severely handicapped.

Once seated, the audience did not wait quietly and patiently. Even amongst the wealthy people fights were frequent. When every gentleman wore a sword, these fights could be serious. Equally serious for the play was the fact that seats on the apron stage were sold to members of the audience. Often these were bought by young men who did not hesitate to interrupt the play with what they thought were humorous remarks.

In the early years of the eighteenth century all the theatres in the City of Westminster were placed under the control of the Lord Chamberlain. Every play had to be passed by him. Originally this was to prevent plays being written against the Government. This power was later extended to cover all plays in the whole country, and lasted until 1968 when the censorship was abolished.

During this period, a famous actor, David Garrick, did much for the theatre. He refused to allow anyone on the stage except the actors, and he engaged soldiers from the Guards to keep order in the auditorium.

38   *Two Guardsmen ejecting an unruly member of the audience.*

It is with three comedies, produced between 1773 and 1777, that the theatre of the next one hundred and fifty years may be said to have begun. The author of two of them, Sheridan, not only wrote two of the best comedies in the English language – he rebuilt Drury Lane Theatre. It was designed to hold 3,600 people, which made it a very large theatre. As it could only be lit by candles or oil lamps, those people furthest from the stage could have seen very little.

Sheridan's two comedies are important because they are plays in which the characters talk naturally. Previously, natural speech was rarely heard on the stage, lines being recited in a loud voice. This use of natural speech had its effect on the design of the theatre.

Drury Lane was really much too large for this kind of acting. It is still too large today. The intimate, natural acting required by plays of this type is only effective in a much smaller theatre. In such a theatre, the audience is near enough to the actors to feel that they know them. It is impossible really to feel in sympathy with a man who is shouting at you from a great distance.

So once again, the popular play of the day influenced the design of the theatre in which it was acted. There were also, of course, larger theatres for opera and ballet.

The words of a Sheridan play were lost in the vast auditorium of Drury Lane in 1777.

The nineteenth century, from about 1820 onwards, saw great changes in the equipment of the theatre. Some of these were due to the introduction of better lighting, which you may read about on page 50 of this book. Apart from lighting, much was done to make the scenery on the stage seem more real.

The destruction by fire of the two chief London theatres, Covent Garden in 1808 and Drury Lane in the following year, made it possible to replace them with more up-to-date buildings. In the course of the century, more facilities were added, especially in the setting of the plays.

The painted back-cloth, which had often had tables and chairs painted on it, was replaced in 1860 by what is known as the box set: that is, a room with solid-looking walls, proper doors and a ceiling. Machinery was introduced to enable stages to sink or revolve, and scenery to be changed quickly. By the end of the century, a forest on the stage really looked like a forest.

Queen Victoria began to take an interest in the theatre. The better-class people who had deserted it at the beginning of the century, came back. One result was the installation of upholstered seats in the stalls and dress circle. The pit, pushed further and further back, still had backless forms for seating. The old apron stage completely disappeared, to be replaced by a narrow orchestra pit.

Elaborate stage machinery in a Victorian theatre.

The stage is shown cut-away to reveal machinery. Apart from the moving tracks to keep the running horses stationary whilst running, the fence supports also moved backwards and the painted backcloth flashed past behind. Man in wings controlled speed.

In 1800, there were ten theatres in London; fifty years later there were more than forty. This was partly due to the Industrial Revolution, which doubled the population of Greater London. Another reason was the difference in the type of audience in the first half of the century.

The more cultured section of the population lost interest in the theatre. The music halls became more popular, but with a different class of people. They developed from the musical entertainments in taverns where the audience sat at tables, smoking and drinking. When the managers found that this was what a large section of the public wanted, large music halls were built. The audience came mainly from the working class.

However, the same type of audience also began to request a lurid type of play which they could understand, and out of this demand grew the melodrama of the first half of the century. A melodrama is a drama with music. The audiences insisted on action and novelty, and the stage had to supply the demand. Floods and fires, Indians and cowboys, shipwrecks and crime stories, and even elephants and camels provided the excitement which today is supplied by television and the cinema.

Out of the scenic and mechanical advances of these melodramas grew the theatre of the beginning of the twentieth century. At theatres like His Majesty's and The Lyceum this meant very costly and elaborate scenery.

A music hall of the nineteenth century.

Two world wars put an end to the lavish setting of plays. Everything became too expensive. Except in the case of large, chiefly American, musical entertainments and ballet, the theatre began to look for its effects in simplicity. A few platforms, some steps and a couple of pillars set against a blue sky became common, if often unsuitable, settings for many plays.

A great influence in the early days of the new type of setting was Gordon Craig. In 1911, he staged a production of *Hamlet*, using only screens as scenery. It was not a success. But he continued to design sets which were never built, as well as sets which were. He was also an early believer in the importance of lighting not so much the actors, but queer and often very large, oddly-shaped blocks of solid material.

Out of this sort of experimental work grew many of the settings of the second half of the century. The proscenium arch was also abandoned. In fact, after two thousand years, the theatre went back to many of the stage conventions of Ancient Greece and Rome; but there was a difference: the use of artificial lighting could now be directed and controlled.

The desire to experiment grew quite out of control. Theatre in the round, with nothing more than a few chairs– or none, the theatre of the absurd, the theatre of this and that struggled, withered and died, except for plays written expressly for it.

A performance on an open stage, with the audience on three sides.

Today, lighting plays a very large and important part in the settings and effects offered by the experimental theatre. How did it all start, and how has it developed?

From the time of the Greek theatre, about 400 B.C., to the days of Shakespeare, lighting presented no problems. It was free, because all plays took place in daylight.

With the covered tennis courts and the specially built theatres of Charles II, some sort of artificial light became necessary. Only candles, torches and simple oil lamps were available. For the more elaborate masques at Court they were already in use. Even coloured light was most ingeniously arranged. In Italy light was directed through glass bottles filled with clear, coloured liquid; in England, in Charles I's time, frames with stretched, coloured silk were used. Coloured light obtained in this way must have been very dim.

The trouble with lamps and candles was that once they were out, for example during a night scene, they could not be relit quickly. Not that night scenes were ever very effective, because the auditorium was lit by clusters of candles hung from the roof, and these were kept alight all through the play. Candles also needed to be snuffed when the wicks became charred. This was done by attendants who moved freely about the stage or in the auditorium, snuffing the candles as required. No-one took any notice of them.

A candle snuffer at work during a performance in the days of Charles II.

Footlights, or 'floats' as they are still called in the theatre, were first installed in 1660 in a theatre at Dorset Gardens built by Davenant. They were called floats because they actually floated. To avoid the danger of fire, the candles were in small basins which floated in a long trough full of water.

The lighting of stages must always have been bad until the coming of gas soon after 1800. Not only was gaslight much better, it could be controlled from a central board. In some of the old provincial theatres such a control board may still be seen. All the pipes to footlights, battens, etc., were separately turned on or off, or dimmed as desired, from one place, usually just behind the proscenium.

A row of gas footlights was very hot indeed. As the grease paint used by the actors was often home-made, it used to melt and run down their faces. Some of the villains must have looked very fierce indeed! In 1860 the first 'limes' were introduced. These consisted of a jet of oxy-hydrogen gas directed on a small cylinder of a lime-like substance, producing a spot of intensely bright light.

Electric lighting came to the Savoy Theatre, London, in 1880, and a new stage era may be said to have begun. This form of lighting was safe and flexible. Realistic settings and effects were now practicable, as well as infinite possibilities for experiments in the future.

A modern stage setting for 'Macbeth'.

A Ladybird Book
Series 662